First Readers' Club

This book was first read by:

Katie Borlee

Grade: 4 A   Date: 11/22/11

Nora and the Texas Terror

Chapter books by Judy Cox

NORA

AND THE

TEXAS TERROR

by **Judy Cox**

illustrated by
Amanda Haley

Holiday House / New York

Library of Congress Cataloging-in-Publication Data
Cox, Judy.
Nora and the Texas terror / by Judy Cox ; illustrated by Amanda Haley. — 1st ed.
p. cm.
Summary: When Nora's uncle loses his job and house in Texas, he and his family
come to stay with Nora's family in Portland, Oregon, and Nora must try very hard
to adjust to her cousin Ellie, who is loud, stubborn, and a tease.
ISBN 978-0-8234-2283-8 (hardcover)
[1. Cousins—Fiction. 2. Family life—Oregon—Fiction. 3. Schools—Fiction.
4. Individuality—Fiction.] I. Haley, Amanda, ill. II. Title.
PZ7.C83835Nn 2010
[Fic]—dc22
2010014329

To Tim,
Thanks for the funny bits.
J. C.

To my dear friend Tina B.
We had fun, didn't we?
A. H.

Contents

1
The Haunted House

The October wind tugged at Nora's clothes. It ruffled her hair. It snatched at her backpack. Nora didn't mind the wind. She splashed through puddles as she walked home from the bus stop with her best friend, Lisette. They sang words to the chicken dance from the third grade music program.

They stopped when they reached the empty house. "Never, never walk past that house," whispered Lisette. The girls crossed the street so they could view the house from a safe distance.

The house stood on the corner next to Nora's house. It was an old house. No curtains hung in the windows. It had a front porch with twisty pillars. Bare trees behind the house swayed in the wind. Their branches looked like bony fingers.

"Do you think it's *really* haunted?" asked Nora, chewing her hair nervously.

"My brother heard the ghost moaning," said Lisette. "And he saw spooky lights, right up there." She pointed to the second-floor window. "*I* think it's the ghost of a lady whose baby died. She can't rest in peace. All night long she wanders through the house crying."

Nora shivered, not sure whether to be scared or thrilled. Piles of unused lumber were stacked nearby. Mounds of red dirt lay heaped in the yard. Underneath the porch was a hole as big as a cave. *The basement*, thought Nora. *I'll bet it's full of spiders*. Just the thought of spiders scuttling through the empty house made her stomach knot. If there was anything Nora hated, it was creepy-crawly spiders.

Lisette lowered her voice to a whisper. "I wouldn't go in there for a million bucks."

Me either, thought Nora. *Not even for two million.*

2
Good News?

Nora said good-bye to Lisette. She ran up her front stairs and flung open the door. "I'm home!" she yelled.

"In here!" called Mom from Nora's bedroom. Baby Kimmy's playpen was set up in the hall. Nora patted Kimmy's head as she went by. Kimmy blew a spit bubble. Nora wanted to tell Mom about her day. But she forgot all about it when she saw her room.

Her room looked completely different. Her dresser was pushed into a corner. Her bed was under the window. A folding bed was set up next to it. Mom was tucking in blankets. She smiled when Nora came in.

"What's that bed for?" Nora asked. The extra bed took up a lot of space. Where would she practice ballet?

"Good news!" said Mom. She pushed her long

brown hair—hair that looked just like Nora's—out of her eyes and smiled. "Aunt Becca and Uncle Chad are coming! And bringing your cousins!"

Nora let her backpack slide to the floor. "Ellie and Ryan?" she asked. She had only seen her cousins once, at a family reunion. For years the two families had planned to visit each other. But times were tight (as Mom always said). Ellie lived in Texas and Nora in Oregon. Too expensive to visit. "We'll go someday," Mom often said. But somehow, someday never came.

"Are they coming for a vacation?" Nora asked. October was a strange time for a vacation.

Mom frowned. "Not exactly a vacation," she said slowly. "They are going to stay with us until they get on their feet."

"What's that mean?" Nora asked, picturing her cousins in their stocking feet.

But Mom went on. "Aunt Becca and Uncle Chad will have the room over the garage. The sofa folds out into a bed. I borrowed a cot for Ryan. He'll sleep up there, too."

"But that's where we watch TV," said Nora. "And it's going to be Kimmy's room when she gets bigger."

Mom laughed. "She won't need it for a while, honey. You can watch TV in the living room. We'll adjust."

"Where's Ellie going to sleep?" asked Nora uneasily. She thought she knew what was coming.

"I thought it would be nice for Ellie to share your room," said Mom. "It will give you girls a chance to get to know one another!"

That was what Nora was afraid of.

Kimmy began to whine. "Feeding time," said Mom. She picked up Kimmy, leaving the playpen in the hall.

Nora sat on her bed. She emptied her backpack. One, two, three library books. She stacked them neatly on top of her bookcase next to her sparkly pink diary.

Usually, Nora dove right into her books on library day. She liked to read one chapter of each book before deciding which one to read first. But Nora didn't feel like reading today.

Ellie coming to stay was *not* good news. The only time the two families had met was three years ago, but Nora remembered Ellie all too well.

Mom and Aunt Becca were sisters, but they didn't look alike. Nora remembered Aunt Becca as a pretty blonde lady who smelled like cinnamon. Uncle Chad had a red beard and sang silly songs. She'd be excited to see them. She'd even be happy to see Ellie's little brother, Ryan, again.

But Ellie! Nora pulled a strand of hair into her

mouth and chewed on it. The last time she'd seen Ellie, Nora had been five years old. Ellie was five, too. Ryan was one. Kimmy hadn't been born yet.

At the reunion, Ellie had raced around the room like a Texas twister. "Listen to me! I'm a fire engine!" she yelled. "WOOOO-WOOOO-WOOOO!"

Nora had heard a grown-up say, "That child is a terror."

Nora had stood by the refreshment table, carefully holding a paper cup of punch. Ellie had bumped into her. Red punch had spilled down the front of Nora's new white sundress. The sundress she'd been so proud of.

Nora had started to cry, and Ellie had pulled hair. "Crybaby!" she'd teased.

Nora hadn't seen Ellie since. Just cards at birthdays and Christmas, phone calls and home videos. Nora hoped Ellie had changed.

But she didn't think so.

3
The Texas Terror

The cousins arrived just before dinner on Sunday. Nora saw the car pull up out front. "They're here!" she shouted. In spite of her worry about Ellie, she couldn't wait. She flung open the front door. She dashed down the porch stairs and into Aunt Becca's arms.

"Nora!" Aunt Becca hugged her. "Let me look at you!" She held Nora at arm's length. Nora got a good look at her, too. Aunt Becca was as fair as Mom was dark. She wore her short blonde hair spiked up. Three earrings sparkled in each earlobe. A sprinkle of freckles dusted her nose.

Nora didn't have time to see more, because Uncle Chad picked her up. "My, my, how you've grown!" he said in his soft Texas drawl. He swung her around. He wore a plaid shirt, jeans, and cowboy boots. Nora was disappointed that he didn't wear a cowboy hat. Instead, he wore a blue Texas Rangers ball cap. He put Nora down and shook Dad's hand. "I can't tell y'all how much we appreciate this," he said.

"Not at all," Dad said. "What are families for?"

Just then, the car door flew open.

"Incoming!" someone hollered, and a soccer ball blasted out, missing Nora's head by inches.

Ellie slid out of the backseat. "Gotta be quick!" Ellie said. "Should have blocked that shot."

Ellie was taller than Nora. Her short blonde hair looked just like Aunt Becca's. A spray of freckles peppered her nose, too. She wore a blue T-shirt that read Don't Mess with Texas. Nora halfway expected her to make siren noises, but she just grinned.

Nora blinked, not sure if she should hug her cousin. But Ellie didn't seem to want a hug. Instead, Ellie slugged Nora in the shoulder, not too hard, but hard enough.

"Howdy," she drawled. She had a Texas accent, too. "Long time no see."

"Not long enough," Nora muttered, rubbing her shoulder.

Mom came down the steps holding Kimmy.

"Get a look at these girls!" Aunt Becca called to her. "Sunshine and shadow! Just like we were!"

"We're so glad you came!" Mom said. Aunt Becca took Kimmy. Mom gave her sister a hug.

"Don't forget me!" Ryan climbed out of his car seat. His pale yellow hair was cut so short that it looked transparent. He wore cowboy boots like his dad's.

Ryan grabbed Nora's hand. "I'm a grrraffe," he announced. He sounded like Uncle Chad. "Do y'all know that grrraffe's have long necks?"

Nora was delighted. When she was little, she liked to pretend to be animals, too. Sometimes, in private, she still did. "Don't you mean a giraffe?" she asked.

"No," said Ryan. He shook his head seriously. "I'm a grraffe because I go *grrrr*. Wanna play grrraffe with me?"

"Sure!" Nora grinned.

"But first, I have t'go," Ryan said, pulling her toward the house. "Where's the bafroom? Grraffe has t'go *now!*"

When Nora and Ryan came back out, Uncle Chad and Dad were unloading the car. Mom and Aunt Becca stood on the steps, talking. Ellie rocked on the porch swing, dragging her heels. She stood up when Nora came out.

"I hope you like animals," she said, with a sly look. "Because I brought Fuzzy."

"Who's Fuzzy?" asked Nora. Ryan let go of her hand. He hopped down the steps to his mom.

Uncle Chad slammed the trunk. "That's it for now," he said. "We can bring in the rest after dinner."

"Who's Fuzzy?" repeated Nora. "A hamster?"

"Nope. Not a hamster." Ellie laughed.

"A guinea pig?"

Ellie shook her head. "You'll just have to wait and see, won't you?"

"It's not a rat, is it?" asked Nora. "I hate rats."

Ellie just laughed. Then she narrowed her eyes. "Are you still a crybaby?" she teased. "I'll bet you're a big ol' scaredy-cat, too." She poked Nora in the chest with her finger. "I just know you are gonna *love* Fuzzy."

Nora could tell she didn't mean it. She hasn't changed one bit, thought Nora as she followed everyone into the house. She's still a terror.

4
Spaghetti—but No Meatballs

Dinner was like a party. Everyone talked at once. The table was so small that Nora had to hold her elbows in. But no one else seemed to mind.

"I wanna sit by Nora!" demanded Ryan.

"He's taken quite a shine to you," said Uncle Chad.

Nora grinned. She'd always wanted a younger brother. Kimmy was still too little to play with.

Mom had made a big pot of spaghetti and meatballs.

"No meatballs for me," Nora reminded Mom as she dished up. "I only like sauce and noodles."

Ellie made a face. "No spaghetti noodles for me. I only like sauce and meatballs."

Aunt Becca laughed. She passed the plate to Ellie. "Just like us at that age! Remember?" she said to Mom. They began reminiscing. Nora ate her noodles, rolling them up on the fork as she listened to the grown-ups talk.

"How's Dad?" asked Aunt Becca. Nora knew they were talking about Grandpa, not her father. Grandpa was Mom and Aunt Becca's dad.

Mom passed around a plate of French bread. "He's still on the coast. When he gets back to Portland, we'll go visit. Won't he enjoy having us all so close!"

"That's one silver lining anyhow," said Aunt Becca. For a moment, she looked sad.

"How's the job hunt going?" Dad asked Uncle Chad. Nora realized, with a shock, that Uncle Chad was out of work.

"I have an interview in the morning," said Uncle Chad.

Ryan picked at his spaghetti. "Aunt Ruthie, grraffe's don't eat 'paghetti. We eat leaves. Don't you have any leaves?" he whined.

"He's overtired," said Aunt Becca. "It's been a long day."

"Long month, you mean," muttered Ellie, stabbing a meatball with her fork.

After dinner, everyone pitched in to clean up. Ellie and Nora cleared the table. Dad and Uncle

Chad loaded the dishwasher. Mom cleaned up Kimmy. Aunt Becca put away the leftovers. Nora was amazed at how fast everything got done with so many helpers.

Ryan yawned. Ellie handed him an animal cracker. "He only eats the lions," she said.

"I bite their heads off," said Ryan. "So they can't bite me." He yawned again. Uncle Chad picked him up and headed to the stairs.

"He'd better have a bath and an early night," Aunt Becca said, following.

"I want Nora to tuck me in!" yelled Ryan.

"Would you mind?" Aunt Becca asked.

Nora grinned, delighted. "I'll read you a bed-time story," she told him. She ran to her room and came back with *Goodnight Moon*.

"Perfect," said Aunt Becca. "That's his favorite."

"That's a baby book," Ellie muttered.

Nora stuck out her chin. She wasn't going to let Ellie spoil her evening. "Is not," she whispered.

"Is so," Ellie whispered back. A look from Aunt Becca made them stop.

After reading to Ryan, Nora and Dad helped Uncle Chad and Ellie finish unloading the car. It didn't take long.

"Most of our stuff is in storage in Texas," said Ellie. She hauled a big duffle bag into Nora's room. She dropped it on the new bed. "We had to store everything when we lost the house." She unzipped the bag and pulled out a soccer ball.

How could you lose a house, Nora wondered. *Surely houses were too big to lose? And weren't they rooted to the spot, like trees or something?*

"What do you mean?" she asked.

Ellie didn't answer right away. "It's so weird that you don't have any pets," she said, pulling out a framed photo. "These are my dogs, Bubba and Sue. Bubba's the black lab. Sue's part Irish setter, part border collie, and part we-don't-know-what." She set the photograph carefully on the bookcase next to Nora's diary. "When my dad lost his job, we couldn't make the house payments anymore so the bank took it back."

Homeless! Nora gasped. Now she understood what Mom meant about it not being a vacation. They had no place to live.

Ellie didn't look at her. She just kept pulling clothes out of her duffle bag and dropping them on the bed. "The worst part was leaving Bubba and Sue behind. Our friends in Texas are keeping them."

"That's awful!" exclaimed Nora. How horrible it must be to leave your pets. She wanted a kitten, but Mom kept saying she had to wait until Kimmy was older.

Ellie stopped pulling out clothes. She put her fists on her hips and glared at Nora. "You don't have to feel sorry for us," she said. "My dad will get a job and a place to live and the first thing we'll do is go get Bubba and Sue and bring them home."

For a moment, Nora thought she saw Ellie's eyes brim with tears, but then Ellie grinned.

"Anyway, Dad bought me a new pet. A pet I can take with me anywhere—Fuzzy."

Just then, Uncle Chad brought in a towel-covered bundle. He set it down on Nora's desk. "Can't leave Fuzzy in the car!" he said. "She likes it warm."

He looked around the room and smiled. "You girls will be as snug as two peas in a pod in here," he said. "Make it an early night, ladies. No late night gabfests!" He left the room, singing "Good-Night, Ladies" in his deep voice.

Nora eyed the towel-covered bundle suspiciously.

"Are you ready to meet Fuzzy?" Ellie asked.

"Say hello to your new roommate!" Ellie yelled. She swept off the towel. "Heeeeere's Fuzzy!"

At first, the glass tank looked empty. Nora saw dirt and a small hollow log. Then she saw a flicker of movement. A giant spider!

5
Fuzzy

Nora stared at the spider, unable to tear her eyes away. She absolutely hated, despised, and detested spiders. How could she share her room with one?

The spider was as big as Nora's hand. Coarse brown hair. Eight thick, furry legs. A fat body. And were those fangs? She shuddered.

Suddenly the spider scuttled over to the side of the tank. It reared up on its hind legs and tapped two front legs against the glass, almost as if it were reaching for Nora. Nora jumped.

Ellie mistook her horrified gaze for interest. "Fuzzy is a Chilean rose hair tarantula," she said proudly. "Isn't she sweet? I feed her live crickets once a week." She picked up a plastic container and shook it. Immediately the room filled with chirping.

Live crickets! Gross! "Can it get—" Nora's voice

cracked. She swallowed and tried again. "Can it get out of the tank?"

Ellie tapped the mesh screen on top of the tank. "Chilean rose hair tarantulas shouldn't be handled too much. They are very delicate."

"But aren't tarantulas poisonous?" Nora's skin prickled. She felt sick to her stomach.

Ellie shot her a disgusted look. "Venomous, you mean. Poisonous is something you eat. Like toadstools. Venomous is something that bites you. Like spiders and snakes. Yeah, tarantulas are venomous. But their bite isn't dangerous. It's like a bee sting. It hurts, but it won't kill you."

She leaned down to peer into the tank. "Hi, Fuzzy, sweetie!" She made kissing noises at the spider. "People used to think that your bite was deadly. Isn't that silly?"

Nora couldn't believe Ellie talked to a spider—and baby talk, too!

Aunt Becca opened the door. "Bedtime, girls. It's a school night." She hugged Nora. "This may turn out to be a blessing in disguise. A chance to get to know my niece!"

Mom came in behind Aunt Becca. "I was going to say the same thing!" she said, wrapping Ellie and Nora in a hug. "Isn't this fun! Like a sleepover!"

Later, Nora lay awake in the dark. She couldn't sleep. That thing in the tank bothered her. Didn't spiders have eight eyes? She'd read that some-where. She could feel the tarantula staring at her with all eight eyes. She squeezed her own two eyes shut.

From the room over the garage, Ryan wailed, "I don't wanna go to bed!" She heard Uncle Chad singing a lullaby.

There were unfamiliar sounds in her room, too. Chirping crickets. And a dry tapping—*was that Fuzzy crawling up the side of the tank? Trying to escape?* Nora shivered. *What if it did get out? What if it crawled on her! How could she sleep in the same room with a giant spider?*

For a moment, she considered complaining to her parents. But if she did, Ellie would call her a scaredy-cat. She pulled her blanket up over her head. *I'm no tattletale*, she thought. *Not one bit.*

Before she finally drifted off to sleep, she heard a new sound. Like someone crying.

Was that Ellie? Nora sat up. "Are you okay?" she whispered. "Do you want me to get your mom?"

There was no answer. But the crying—if it was crying—stopped.

6
Peanut Butter—but No Jelly

Nora woke up before Ellie the next morning. She flung off her blanket. She tiptoed over to Fuzzy's cage, relieved to see the screen still in place. Fuzzy wasn't visible. She must be hiding in the hollow log. Nora didn't want to see the tarantula, but she couldn't stop herself from looking.

Ellie slept soundly, curled up in a tangle of blankets. Her bare toes poked out of the end of the bed.

Nora wrote in her diary, as she did every morning. Then she pulled on pants and a pink sweater and went into the kitchen. Mom was in her bathrobe, feeding Kimmy strained bananas.

Dad stood at the counter, making coffee. Nora thought he looked handsome in the suit and tie he wore for his job at the insurance company. Uncle Chad sat at the table, typing on. This morning he wore a suit and tie, too. He looked more like a grown-up than he had yesterday, but he kept pulling on his collar as if it itched.

Aunt Becca wasn't downstairs yet, but Nora could hear Ryan. "I don't wanna get up!"

Nora opened the cupboard. She pulled out a bowl and a box of cereal. It wasn't her usual kind.

"Where's my cereal?" she asked.

Mom shook her head. "Times are tight," she said. "This brand is cheaper." Nora made a face as she poured it into her bowl.

The party feeling from last night was gone. Now it was just grown-ups and grumpy kids. Like the morning after a sleepover when everyone is tired and cranky.

Nora liked routine. Even the pink sweater she wore was her usual Monday sweater. She didn't like surprises. She didn't like her house full of other people. She didn't like change. Not one bit.

Ellie came in, rubbing the sleep out of her eyes. She wore shorts and a red T-shirt that read Soccer Girls Rule.

Mom shook her head. "Shorts in October? Not in Portland, honey," she said. "It's supposed to rain again today. You'll be too cold."

Ryan thumped down the stairs. Aunt Becca followed. Ryan's hair stuck up all over his head, like wispy yellow feathers. He ran over to Nora and hugged her. "I was hoping you were still here," he said. Nora laughed.

"Oh, dear," said Aunt Becca when she saw Ellie. "I wasn't thinking. It's still warm in Texas this time of year. All of our winter clothes are in storage."

"I'm sure Nora has something Ellie can wear," said Mom. "Go look, girls."

In her room, Nora dug through her dresser and pulled out a pink sweatshirt. Ellie scowled as she looked at the ballerina on the front. "Don't you have anything else?" she asked. "Sharks? Tigers? Something fierce?"

Nora shook her head. She had sweatshirts with butterflies or ballerinas and a purple sweater with a dancing mouse.

One by one, Ellie dropped the clothes on the floor. She made a face. "I should have known. You're a girly girl. Miss Priss. I'll bet you don't even own anything black."

"And you're a tomboy," said Nora. "And a Goth."

Ellie put her fists on her hips. "Who ya callin' Goth? *I'm* a Texas girl. My soccer team wore black uniforms. With skulls and crossbones."

Nora nodded. "Goth. I knew it."

"No! We were the Ridgeville Raiders. When you played the Raiders you knew you were in *trou-ble*," she boasted.

"Why don't you wear your uniform then, if it's so great." Nora picked up the scorned shirts and folded them neatly.

Ellie looked wistful. "I had to leave it at school. If you're not in Texas, you can't be a Ridgeville Raider anymore." She pulled on Nora's ballerina sweatshirt.

"Don't laugh," she told her father when she came into the kitchen. Uncle Chad hid his grin behind his coffee mug.

"I'm making sandwiches," said Aunt Becca. "How about peanut butter and jelly, Nora?"

"No peanut butter for me," said Nora. "I only like cream cheese and jelly."

Ellie made a face. "And you know I don't like jelly, Mom!" she said. "Only peanut butter for me."

When the sandwiches were done, Nora handed Ellie a paper bag.

"What's this for?" asked Ellie.

"To pack your lunch in," Nora told her.

Ellie shook her head. "I never use paper bags," said Ellie. "They get soggy. I only take my lunch in plastic bags."

"Plastic bags are bad for the environment." Nora put her sandwich in the bag. "We only use paper bags at our house."

"That's stupid," said Ellie. She scowled. "You can reuse the same plastic bag. So that's better for the environment than paper bags because you don't cut down any trees."

"You're wrong," said Nora. "Paper can be recycled, and plastic bags use oil. I'll never take my lunch in a plastic bag."

"Well, I won't use paper bags!" insisted Ellie.

"Stubborn as a team of mules," said Uncle Chad, sipping his coffee.

7
A Bad Start

Nora usually rode the bus to school, but today Aunt Becca drove. "I need to enroll Ellie," she said. "And I want to sign up to substitute teach." Like Nora's mom, Aunt Becca was a teacher. Mom was on family leave until Kimmy was older.

The neighborhood streets looked shiny after last night's rain. "Everything's so green!" exclaimed Aunt Becca. "I'd forgotten how green Oregon is."

"Too green," said Ellie, staring out the window. "Bo-ring. And is the sky always this gray? I call that depressing." She turned to Nora. "In Texas, the sun shines all the time and the sky is blue and there's a lot of it. You can see for miles and miles because there aren't all these stupid trees in the way."

Nora made a face at her cousin. "What's wrong with trees? I'd rather have trees than cactus." Nora was getting sick of hearing about Texas.

"Shows how much you know," said Ellie. "Texas has way better trees than this."

"Girls!" warned Aunt Becca. The girls were silent for the rest of the trip.

It was so early that none of the buses had arrived yet. Aunt Becca parked the car, and they all walked into the school.

Ellie was in third grade, too. "I'm in Mr. Baldwin's class," Nora told Ellie as they followed Aunt Becca to the office. "He's my favorite teacher. He's always making jokes. You'll probably be in Miss Saldivar's class. Or maybe Mrs. Pruitt's class."

Ellie just shrugged.

"Nora, hon." Aunt Becca opened the office door. "You'll help Ellie get on the right bus after school, won't you?"

Nora nodded. She used to go to ballet class on Monday afternoons. But Mom said the lessons were too expensive. So now she rode the bus home, as she did the other days.

"I guess I'll see you at lunch," said Ellie in a tight voice. She didn't sound like her usual spunky self. *Was the Texas terror scared? Impossible!*

Nora knew she'd be frightened to start a new school. She'd been going to Bybee Elementary forever. She knew all the teachers and most of the kids. For just a moment, Nora felt sorry for Ellie.

"Don't worry," she told her cousin. "The kids here are pretty nice."

"I'm not worried!" said Ellie. She scowled. "They better not mess with me is all."

Nora rolled her eyes. If Ellie wanted to be a grouch, Nora wouldn't let it spoil her day. She hurried down the hall to her classroom. It was a relief to be in familiar territory. *Her* teacher. *Her* friends. *Her* books. No weird cousins. And no spiders!

The bell rang, and the kids took their seats. Nora just had time to sit down, when the classroom door opened. All the kids looked up.

Ms. Whitestone, the principal, came in. "You have a new student, Mr. Baldwin," said Ms. Whitestone. "Everyone, please welcome Ellie Baxter. Ellie is Nora's cousin from Texas." Ellie came in.

Mr. Baldwin smiled. He led Ellie over to Nora's desk. "Times are tight," he said. "So it will be a few days before we can get another desk. Luckily, you can share with Nora."

Nora slid her chair over as far as she could. Mr. Baldwin scooted another chair beside Nora. Ellie sat down. Ellie's legs were so long that Nora had to scrunch up to keep from touching her. Ellie seemed to have regained her spunk, because she grinned and bumped Nora's knees. *On purpose!* Nora looked away.

"Two cousins with the same name!" Mr. Baldwin chuckled. "I'll bet that doesn't happen every day."

What did Mr. Baldwin mean? Nora wondered. Her last name was Robinson and Ellie's was Baxter. She slid her eyes to Ellie, but Ellie shrugged. Clearly, she didn't know what Mr. Baldwin meant either.

But there wasn't time to ask. Mr. Baldwin signaled everyone to stand for the Pledge of Allegiance.

The whole morning was pure misery. Ellie kept bumping Nora's knees. She peeked at Nora's work. She borrowed Nora's pencils without asking. When Mr. Baldwin called Blake's name, Ellie whispered loudly, "Is he your crush?" The kids snickered. Nora blushed.

How does she know that? wondered Nora. She'd never told anyone, not even Lisette. She'd only written it in her diary yesterday. *Had Ellie read . . . ? No, even Ellie wouldn't do such a thing!*

When the bell rang for recess, Lisette came over. "Cute sweatshirt," she told Ellie.

Ellie scowled. "*This?*" she asked. She pulled the hem of the shirt out and scowled at the ballerina. "It's not mine. *She's* the ballet dork!" She stabbed her thumb in Nora's direction.

At least Nora didn't have to play with Ellie at recess. Ellie ran out to the playground and joined a soccer game. Nora and Lisette made elf houses in the grass, as they always did. They made leaf beds and acorn cap dishes. Across the field, Nora watched Ellie chase the black-and-white ball.

"She'd better not get my sweatshirt dirty," Nora told Lisette. But a few minutes later, Ellie slid on the wet grass. When she got up, Nora's pink sweatshirt was splattered with mud.

"Figures," muttered Nora.

After recess, Nora stood behind Ellie in line to use the drinking fountain. "Wanna see how we cool off in Texas?" Ellie put her finger over the faucet. Water sprayed over the fountain, drenching Nora. "Gotcha!" said Ellie.

In the classroom, Mr. Baldwin looked at Nora. "Do you need to use the bathroom?" he asked kindly.

Nora looked down. Water had darkened the front of her pants. Mr. Baldwin thought she'd wet her pants! She sank into her chair. She buried her head in her arms, certain that everyone was laughing.

What a way to start the week!

8

Stay on Your Own Side!

That afternoon, Aunt Becca met them at the bus stop. Ryan swung on her hand, hopping up and down on one foot. "How was school?" asked Aunt Becca.

"Okay, I guess," Ellie said.

Nora rolled her eyes. It had been a horrible day, not okay at all. But she wasn't going to tattle. Besides, there was one thing she wanted to know. "Aunt Becca, why did Mr. Baldwin say Ellie and I have the same name? Our names don't even sound alike."

There were lots of kids in the third grade with the same names. There were two Marias and three Dylans, each spelled differently: Dylan, Dillon, and Dillan. And sometimes Mr. Baldwin got confused and called the wrong name when he wanted Jasmine, Jamaica, or Jayme. But Ellie Baxter and

Nora Robinson didn't even start with the same letter.

Aunt Becca didn't answer right away. Her cheeks turned pink. "Well, it's a long story," she began. But then they reached the empty house.

"Cross the street," ordered Nora. "Never walk past that house!" She lowered her voice. "It's haunted."

"Let me see!" Ryan leaned over the fence. "A cave!" he said, pointing to the hole under the porch. "Do bears live there?"

"No," said Aunt Becca. "And you are not to go near that place. It could be dangerous."

"Ghosts?" asked Nora. Her voice trembled.

"Construction site," said Aunt Becca. "Holes, nails, broken glass. Looks like someone was remodeling and ran out of money. Besides, it's private property." She took Ryan's hand and led him down the street.

"*I'm* not afraid of ghosts," Ellie told Nora as they followed Aunt Becca. She turned and shook her fist at the house. "Ghosts should be afraid of *me*."

When Nora came into her room after dinner that night, Ellie was sitting on her bed, drawing. Nora's diary—her precious pink sparkly diary—lay on the floor, facedown. Nora picked it up. The pages were bent. One page had been torn out, leaving a ragged edge.

"You sneak!" she cried. "That's my private property!"

Ellie looked up from her drawing. "I didn't read your stupid old diary. Besides, it's not that interesting. I just wanted some paper. To draw a picture of Bubba and Sue."

Nora fought down a small pang of sympathy. It wasn't fair that she had to share her room with Ellie and all her stuff, too. "You could ask first!"

It was suddenly too much to bear. First, her favorite sweatshirt. Then, her favorite teacher. Now, her private diary.

Nora bundled up Ellie's soccer ball, her shorts, her T-shirts, and her shoes. She flung them in a heap on Ellie's folding bed.

She ran to the garage. She grabbed a roll of duct tape and a tape measure from Dad's workbench. Using the tape measure, she carefully measured the width of her bedroom.

"What do you think you're doing?" Ellie asked.

Nora didn't answer. After she had measured the room, she stuck a line of duct tape right down

the middle. Her bed was on one side. Ellie's bed
was on the other.

Nora glared at her cousin. "This is your half of
the room," she said, pointing. "And this is mine.
From now on, keep your stuff on your side!"

9
Ancestor Detectors

The next Tuesday, Mr. Baldwin raised his hand to get everyone's attention. "Good news!" he said. "It's time for a new project!"

Nora's eyes shone. Mr. Baldwin's projects were always fun. Once, they made a volcano with baking soda and vinegar. Another time, they built a cave out of a huge cardboard box. They learned about cave explorers called spelunkers.

"This month, we'll be digging into family history," Mr. Baldwin continued. "You'll be ancestor detectors. Each student will make a family tree with the names of your parents, your grandparents, and your sisters and brothers. You can add your aunts and uncles, even great-aunts and uncles, if you like. And your cousins, too." He winked at Ellie and Nora.

Mr. Baldwin held up a chart that looked like a

tree, with little spaces for names on the branches. "After you make your family tree, I want you to pick a relative—not parents or aunts and uncles. Somebody older. And interview them."

Mr. Baldwin showed them a booklet. "Write your interview in here. This includes some questions you can ask. Finally, you'll give an oral report to the class." He chuckled. "We'll see what kind of roots you've sprouted from!"

Ellie's hand shot up. "Do we have to?" she asked, to make kids laugh. *Smart aleck!* Nora rolled her eyes.

Mr. Baldwin ignored Ellie. He handed out the family tree charts and interview booklets. But there weren't enough to go around.

"I'll share with Lisette," said Nora. "We can be partners." Lisette nodded eagerly.

But Mr. Baldwin shook his head. "No. I want you to work with Ellie since you are cousins. Find out what relatives you have in common—maybe grandparents? Perhaps you can interview one of them."

Nora was about to protest. But Mr. Baldwin held up his hand. "It'll be good for you," he said, as he moved down the row of desks. *Now they not only had to share a desk, they had to share their project!*

At lunchtime, Ellie took her peanut butter sandwich over to Jake and Holly, her soccer friends. Nora sat next to Lisette at their usual table. She nibbled her cream cheese and jelly sandwich, leaving the crusts in a tidy pile. She didn't like crusts. She sipped her chocolate milk through two straws, just as she always did. Across the aisle, Ellie belched loudly.

Nora was embarrassed. "She's so rambunctious," she told Lisette, using a word Dad sometimes called her.

"But it must be fun having your cousins live with you," said Lisette, "like a pajama party every night."

Nora made a face. "Well, Aunt Becca and Uncle Chad are great, and Ryan's funny. But Ellie is a terror. She read my diary, I know she did even though she says she didn't. She plays awful jokes. And she brags all the time. Plus, she never stops saying Texas is better. She's too stubborn to admit when she's wrong. And that awful spider!" Nora shuddered.

10

Chili—but No Beans

That night, Mom asked Nora and Ellie to set the table for dinner.

Ellie grinned. "Wanna see how we set the table Texas-style?" she asked Nora. *CRASH*! She dumped all the silverware in a pile in the middle of the table.

"That's not the way," Nora scolded. She picked up the spoons and started to set them in the right places. Carefully.

Ellie watched for a moment, her arms folded, her eyes narrowed. Then she gave a sly little smile. "Where's your armadillo?" she asked.

Nora stopped what she was doing. "Our *what?*"

"Your armadillo. Surely, you have an armadillo?" Ellie shook her head sadly. "I just can't set the table Texas-style without one."

Nora wrinkled her nose. "A *live* armadillo? In Texas, they put *animals* on the table? Yuck!" She could believe anything about someone who kept a giant spider for a pet.

Ellie's eyes danced with mischief. "Gotcha again!" she yelled.

Aunt Becca came in. "Have you seen Ryan? He was here a minute ago," she said. "I told him to pick up his toys before dinner, and he disappeared!"

"I'll look under the beds," said Ellie. "He likes to hide and have somebody find him," she told Nora. They looked in the garage and the bathrooms, but no Ryan. At last, Nora found him in the coat closet, wrapped in Uncle Chad's brown coat.

"I'm a bear in a cave," he said. "Can I eat dinner in here?"

"Sorry, bear," said Nora. "You have to eat at the table with us." She helped him pick up his toys and wash his hands.

At last everyone sat down. Aunt Becca had made a salad. Mom had baked cornbread. Uncle Chad had made chili with beans.

Nora poked at her chili sadly. She didn't like beans. One by one, she scooped out each bean. She hid them under her lettuce. She didn't want to hurt Uncle Chad's feelings.

She looked up. Aunt Becca was watching. She

wasn't mad, though. She laughed. When she laughed, her eyes sparkled like Ellie's.

"Just like when we were kids!" Aunt Becca told Mom. "You never liked beans either!" She smiled at Nora. "That's okay," she said. "You can have a peanut butter and jelly sandwich instead."

"Cream cheese and jelly," Nora reminded her.

"How was school?" asked Dad.

Nora remembered her question. "Why did Mr. Baldwin say Ellie and I have the same name?"

Mom looked at Aunt Becca. Nora thought she looked annoyed. Her brow creased and her lips tightened, just like when Nora was in trouble. And Aunt Becca looked angry, too. She crossed her arms and stuck out her lower lip. But when they caught sight of each other, they both burst out laughing.

Uncle Chad passed the bowl of chili to Dad. Dad took a big scoop. "You sisters certainly take the cake for stubbornness," said Dad.

"That's a fact," said Uncle Chad, grinning.

But no one answered Nora's question. She thought it must be one of the grown-up mysteries that never seem to get answered.

A few days later, Mr. Baldwin reminded the class about the family history projects. "How are my ancestor detectors?" Mr. Baldwin asked the class. "Uncovering any family history mysteries? Don't forget your projects are due at the end of the month."

Nora liked her work to be done on time. In fact, she liked to be the first one to hand in her homework. But all she and Ellie had done so far was to fill in the little blanks on the family tree. Mom and Dad. Aunt Becca and Uncle Chad. Ryan. Kimmy. In the middle, Nora had printed her name neatly. Ellie had scrawled her name in large, wobbly capital letters.

"You're ruining it!" said Nora.

"Am not," said Ellie.

"Are too," said Nora, pulling it away.

"Girls," Mom had warned, "tell you what. I'll call Grandpa. You can interview him for your project."

"Is he my ancestor?" asked Nora.

"Yours and Ellie's both," said Mom.

"He gets home next week," Mom had said when she got off the phone. "He said he'll bake some of his special lasagna," she told Aunt Becca. "In Mom's big blue dish. Remember?" And soon Mom and Aunt Becca were reminiscing again.

Nora didn't care about lasagna or blue dishes. But she couldn't wait to see Grandpa again.

11
Tight Times

On Sunday night, the whole family sat in the living room after dinner. Ellie stared out the window. "All it ever does here is rain," she complained. "In Texas, I play with Bubba and Sue after dinner."

"Wanna play trucks with me?" said Ryan.

"We could play a board game," said Mom. "Or I could teach you how to play Hearts or Crazy Eights." She held out a pack of cards. Ellie shook her head.

"We could rent a DVD," said Dad.

"And pop some popcorn," said Uncle Chad.

"Or how about a jigsaw puzzle?" asked Mom. "We haven't done one in ages."

"Great ideas!" said Aunt Becca. "But before we decide, I have something for the girls." She pulled a shopping bag out of the coat closet. "Ellie needs warmer clothes for school. She can't keep borrowing Nora's! So I went to the thrift store. Look what I found!"

She pulled two sweatshirts out. "One for Ellie and one for Nora. They match!" She handed each girl a sweatshirt.

"Oh, how cute!" said Mom. "Put them on. I can't wait to see them."

"I'll get the camera," said Dad.

Nora and Ellie unfolded their shirts. Each shirt was green with a big orange rabbit on the front.

"Billy Bunny-Wunny!" cried Ryan. "I love Billy Bunny-Wunny! My favorite cartoon show!"

"Ugh!" cried both girls at the same time.

Ellie held her nose. "I *hate* Billy Bunny-Wunny!"

"You *love* Billy Bunny-Wunny," said Uncle Chad.

"That was when I was four!" said Ellie. "I am *so* not wearing this!"

"Me either," said Nora. "I am *so* not wearing this either. People might think we are sisters."

"Who cares about that?" said Ellie. "People will think we are dorks!"

Well, thought Nora. *We agree on one thing.*

Aunt Becca looked disappointed, until Ryan grabbed the shirts where the girls had dropped them. "I want them!" he cried.

They spent the rest of the evening watching Ryan parade around in the Billy Bunny-Wunny

shirts. The arms hung down to the floor. Uncle Chad took pictures.

A few days later, Ellie sat on the floor in front of Fuzzy's tank. She looked worried. "Fuzzy won't eat. I gave her a cricket this morning, but she just lies there. You don't think she's dying, do you?" She turned her anxious face to Nora.

Nora made herself look into the tank. It was clear that something was wrong. Fuzzy lay on her back, completely ignoring the chirping cricket in the tank. Nora shivered. Just looking at the spider made her stomach topsy-turvy.

The next day, the girls argued over what TV show to watch after school. "It's my turn to pick," said Ellie as they walked into the house.

Nora shook her head. "You picked yesterday." Nora dropped her backpack on her side of the room. She stepped over the taped line and went into the kitchen.

Mom was feeding Kimmy. Nora kissed them. She pulled a cheese stick out of the fridge. She grabbed a package of crackers from the cupboard. The same snack, the same routine she followed after every school day.

In the old days (B. E.—Before Ellie), Nora would watch cartoons on the big TV upstairs. But of course that was off-limits now, since Uncle Chad and Aunt Becca were sleeping there. So she and Ellie went into the living room.

Uncle Chad was fiddling with something on top of the TV. "Just a mo'," he said. He twisted some wires behind the TV. Then he stepped back and turned it on. No picture. Just colored lines and static.

"Tight times," he said, scratching the back of his head. "Your folks canceled the cable TV. Too expensive. So they weren't getting any signal. I told them—leave it to me. I'm putting up an antenna. Rabbit ears. Now, if I can just adjust them to pick up the signal. . . ." He went back to work.

The new antenna sat on top of the TV. It did look like a rabbit's ears—if the rabbit were skinny and made of black wire. Uncle Chad pushed it around this way and that. It was almost as much fun to watch him as it was to watch TV. Finally the picture came in sharp and clear.

"There you go!" said Uncle Chad, rubbing his hands on his jeans. "All it took was a little adjustment."

"It's still my turn to pick," Ellie told Nora. "Because yesterday was my turn. But then Aunt Ruthie made us turn it off and go outside. So we didn't get to watch after all. So it's still my turn." She took a bite of her apple.

"No," Nora shook her head. "You get to pick on Mondays, Wednesdays, and Fridays. I get Tuesdays, Thursdays, and Saturdays. No TV on Sundays. Today is Thursday. So it's my turn."

She was just reaching for the remote, when Ryan skipped in, carrying a toy truck. He picked up the remote and flipped to *The Billy Bunny-Wunny Show*.

"My favorite show!" he shouted. "Watch it with me, Daddy!" He and Uncle Chad settled down on the big green couch together.

Nora sighed, and Ellie rolled her eyes. No TV now. *Leave it to little kids to get their own way!*

12
A Tale of Two Sisters

On Saturday, everyone piled into two cars. They couldn't all fit in one. They drove to Grandpa's house. Nora sat in the backseat, next to Kimmy's car seat. Kimmy kept throwing her small stuffed duck on the car floor. Nora had to hand it back. Every time Nora did this, Kimmy laughed and laughed.

Nora liked Grandpa's neighborhood, with its old wooden houses and big trees. The rhododendrons didn't have any flowers on them in October, but the leaves were green and shiny.

Grandpa was standing on the front porch when the cars pulled up to the curb. He had blue eyes like Nora, which twinkled behind his glasses when he saw everyone pile out. Nora ran up the stairs. She gave him a big hug. She'd missed him. She was glad he was back in Portland.

The kitchen filled with people talking, cooking, and setting the table. Nora had that party feeling she'd had when the cousins had first arrived.

After everyone had eaten as much lasagna as he or she could hold, Grandpa got out a banjo.

"Picked this up in Neskowin," he told them. "At a swap meet. It's older than I am and still plays pretty good." He laughed. "Like me!" He strummed a few bars of "Oh, Susannah," and soon everyone was singing along.

When they'd sung their way through a few more songs, Grandpa put down the banjo. "Now, what's all this about a school project?" he asked.

"We have to interview a relative," began Nora.

"Someone old," added Ellie. "I mean, old-*er*," she corrected, after a look from Aunt Becca.

"Well, that's me," said Grandpa. "Older than dirt. What do you want to know?"

"We have a list of questions Mr. Baldwin gave us," said Ellie. She opened the booklet.

But there was one question that wasn't on the list, one question that no one ever seemed to want to answer. Nora had not forgotten.

"Why did Mr. Baldwin say Ellie and I have the same name?" she demanded. "And why won't anyone tell me?"

Grandpa's eyes crinkled up. He laughed until

tears ran down his cheeks. "So you want that story, do you?" he asked.

Aunt Becca tightened her lips. Mom rocked Kimmy, who had fallen asleep. Ryan pushed his toy truck along the rug, making motor noises. Nora looked at Dad and Uncle Chad, leaning back in their chairs and sipping from cans of soda.

Uncle Chad shook his head. "Here it comes," he said. Dad laughed.

Nora looked back at Grandpa.

"I see it's up to me to spill the beans," said Grandpa. He patted the couch. Nora sat on one side. Ellie sat on the other. "Well, as you know, your mothers—Ruth and Rebecca—are sisters," he began.

"Sunshine and shadow, you and Mom used to call us," said Mom, smiling.

"That's right. As close as two sisters can be. Sure, they had their little spats—arguing and making up. Through it all, they were loving and loyal. But a mite high-strung, too!"

All the grown-ups laughed, but Nora tugged Grandpa's sleeve. "Our names, Grandpa?"

"You girls were born two days apart. Nora was born first. Your grandmother, Eleanor, passed away just before you were born." He nodded at Nora. "Ruth wanted to name you Eleanor to honor her.

Problem was, Becca wanted to name her daughter Eleanor, also. Neither one would give in. So they made a pact—a compromise. Each sister would use the name Eleanor, but they'd call one cousin Nora and the other, Ellie."

He stroked his mustache as he looked at the cousins. "I believe you've both inherited your grandmother's stubborn streak. Your mothers have it, too." He chuckled. "Eleanor would have loved you both," he added, looking at the girls.

Nora smiled. Nicknames! Why hadn't she thought of that? Of course she knew her full name was Eleanor, but she hadn't realized that Ellie was short for Eleanor, too.

Grandpa chuckled. "They didn't figure on you girls living in the same house. Or going to the same school.

"I have a photo of your grandmother right here." Grandpa went to the bookshelf. He brought back a framed photograph. The woman in the picture wore an old-fashioned dress. She had Nora's glossy dark hair and Ellie's smiling brown eyes.

"I wish I'd known her," said Nora.

"Me, too," said Ellie. "She looks like fun."

"She had gumption, that lady," said Grandpa.

"What's that mean?" asked Nora.

"Grit," said Grandpa. "Determination. The way

she finished college after having a family. The way she followed me across the country when I was in the army, making us a home in each new place. The way she battled her cancer all the way to the end. I miss her every day of my life."

He set the photo carefully back on the bookshelf and sat back down in his chair. "I understand you've been having some tough times," he said. "I'm told you girls need an attitude adjustment."

Nora thought of the rabbit ears Uncle Chad had

put on the TV to adjust the signal. But Grandpa was still talking.

"Your mothers had tough times, too, growing up. The important thing here is to recognize your kinship. Gumption will get you through this. Love and loyalty will make it worthwhile. Sunshine and shadow—you can't have one without the other. Your moms need each other. And so do you."

Nora smiled politely, but she knew that she and Ellie had nothing more in common than their names. Ellie didn't need her. And she sure didn't need Ellie. Not one bit.

13
A Close Escape

The weeks crept past. Every morning, Dad went to his office at the insurance agency. Uncle Chad went on job interviews. Aunt Becca taught as a substitute, while Mom took care of Ryan and Kimmy.

When Aunt Becca wasn't working, she looked for an apartment. "It's hard to find a place that will take our dogs. Ellie misses them so much. But without permanent jobs, maybe it doesn't make sense to rent a place yet," Nora heard her tell Mom. "When we do find work, we might have to move again."

"You're welcome to stay as long as you need to," said Mom, bouncing Kimmy on her hip.

Nora hoped Uncle Chad would find work soon. It already seemed like Ellie had been there a year. Or two. Or three!

Ellie ignored Nora's taped line. She dropped her things wherever she felt like it. She played loud music when Nora was trying to write in her diary. She lay on her back on the folding bed and bounced her soccer ball off Nora's bedroom wall when Nora wanted to read. She borrowed Nora's clothes without asking. She hogged the bathroom. Every night, Nora had to listen to the sound of chirping crickets.

And, of course, there was Fuzzy. Nora still hid her eyes every time she walked into her room. She didn't want to see the tarantula, even by accident. When Ellie wasn't there, she draped the towel over the tank. She just couldn't get used to having a big, hairy spider living in her room.

At school, Ellie and Nora still shared a desk. "Bear with me, girls," Mr. Baldwin told them. "The new desk is coming from the central warehouse. It should be here soon."

Nora tried to be patient, but things just got worse. One morning, as the class stood up to give the flag salute, Ellie picked up Nora's favorite pencil. The one with pink hearts on it.

"That's mine," hissed Nora. She took it out of Ellie's hand.

"I pledge allegiance," the class recited. No one seemed to notice that Nora and Ellie had not joined in.

"I just need to borrow it for a minute." Ellie grabbed the pencil back. "What's the big deal?"

". . . . To the United States . . . ." recited the class.

"You could ask first," whispered Nora. She pulled, but Ellie didn't let go. Nora and Ellie struggled, having a tug-of-war over the pencil.

"Alright, then," shouted Ellie, "KEEP YOUR OLD PENCIL!" She let go suddenly. Nora lost her balance and sat down, hard, on the floor.

There was a shocked hush. Mr. B hurried over. "Girls!" he said sternly. "That's enough. You owe me ten minutes of recess time for disturbing the class." He shook his head at Nora, as if he were disappointed in her. He wrote their names on the board.

"Gotcha again," whispered Ellie.

Nora's face burned. She had *never* had her name written on the board before! Ooh, that Ellie!

If only she could keep Aunt Becca and Uncle Chad and Ryan. And send Ellie back to Texas.

A few nights later, Nora went to her room. She planned to read in bed. She loved to curl up with a good book. She loved to listen to the rain drumming on the roof. Such a cozy feeling!

But Ellie was already there. She lay on her bed

on her stomach, drawing a picture. Her music was turned up loud.

Ellie's side of the room was a mess, as usual. Her blue T-shirt was wadded up on top of Nora's pillow. Ellie's jeans were draped over Nora's chair. Nora snatched up the clothes.

"Keep your stuff on your own side!" She shook the T-shirt at Ellie. Fuzzy dropped out.

The tarantula landed on Nora's pillow. There it crouched. Brown. Hairy. As big as a clenched fist. Nora screamed. She flung the pillow off the bed.

"Stop!" cried Ellie. "You'll hurt her!" She jumped off the bed. The pillow had landed right

"Stop!" cried Ellie. "You'll hurt her!" She jumped off the bed. The pillow had landed right side up on the floor. The tarantula still clung to the pillowcase.

"Fuzzy!" cried Ellie. "You almost killed Fuzzy!" She knelt on the floor. She gently scooped her spider up in her hands. She put it back in the tank. She put the screen firmly over the top and pounded it down with her fist.

"You put Fuzzy on my pillow on purpose!" Nora's whole body shook. She burst into tears. She'd almost touched a spider!

"I didn't!" shouted Ellie. "I'd never risk hurting Fuzzy! You almost killed her!"

Ryan crept out of the closet where he'd been hiding. He wore cowboy jammies and bunny slippers. "I didn't mean to let it out," he said. "I just wanted to see it close up."

He banged on the glass tank. "Is it dead? It's not moving. I think it's dead. Can I flush it down the toilet like when my goldfish died? Can I?"

"Get lost, Ry-baby!" hollered Ellie. Ryan began to cry.

"Why don't you both go back to Texas where you belong? And take your stupid spider, too!" shouted Nora.

Ellie's face crumpled. "You think I want to be

here, in your dumb old room, in your dumb old house!" she yelled. "I *want* to go home! Back to Texas! Back to Bubba and Sue." Tears ran down her cheeks. "At least *they* love me."

By then, Mom and Aunt Becca had come in. "Children!" said Mom, in her teacher voice.

"I think you'd better sleep upstairs with Ryan tonight," Aunt Becca said. She took Ryan and led him out of the room. Ellie followed without looking back.

"We'll talk about this tomorrow," Mom told Nora. She kissed her good night and turned off the lights. At last, Nora was alone. All alone. Just the way she liked it. *So why did she feel so miserable?*

14

The Storm

The next day, the wind came up. Nora looked out the classroom window. The trees on the playground swayed like dancers bowing. The flag snapped on the flagpole.

All morning, Nora had edged her chair as far from Ellie as she could. But it didn't matter. Ellie didn't try to bump knees. She didn't take Nora's pencils. She didn't talk to Nora at all. She just kept her head down on her desk.

Nora snuck a peek out of the corner of her eyes. Ellie's face was pinched and white. Her freckles stood out like measles. Her eyes were red rimmed as if she'd been crying.

Guilt pricked Nora. She was sorry she hurt Ellie's feelings, and she felt bad for yelling at her. But she still wished Ellie had never come.

By afternoon, the wind was gusting. The roof of

the school rattled. Mr. Baldwin checked his e-mail and called the class together.

"Ms. Whitestone just informed me that a major windstorm is predicted. School will close early. Parents have been contacted. Listen for your name and your instructions."

Mr. Baldwin read the list of which children were being picked up. Which were riding the bus. Which were going to day care. When he called Ellie and Nora's names, he added, "Bus riders, go straight home after the bus lets you off. No dawdling!"

Nora and Ellie grabbed their backpacks. They got in line with the other bus riders.

The wind was howling by the time Nora and Ellie got off the bus. Lisette had been absent, so it was just the two of them. Dark clouds scudded across the sky. Branches snapped as the wind roared through them.

Nora's hair blew into her eyes. She hunched against the gusts, struggling to hold her backpack.

Ellie's eyes shone, and her cheeks were red. She stopped in front of the haunted house and lifted her face to the storm. She flung her arms out.

"You call this a windstorm?" she cried. "Why, in Texas, we have *way* bigger storms than this!"

CRACK! A limb crashed to the ground in front of the house. Nora jumped. "Come on!" hollered Ellie. The girls raced home.

Mom met them at the door. "Thank goodness, you're home! I was worried," she said. She held Kimmy on her hip. Kimmy's face was red, and she was crying. "Kimmy's got a cold," said Mom. She bounced the baby gently. But Kimmy kept fussing.

"Where is everybody?" asked Nora, dropping her backpack.

"Dad's at work," said Mom. "Uncle Chad's at a job interview. Aunt Becca's subbing at a school across town. I hope everyone gets home soon." She looked worried. "In case the roads get blocked with downed trees and power lines."

Nora grabbed some cheese sticks from the fridge. Suddenly, the lights went out. Even though it was afternoon, the cloudy sky made the house dark. It was strangely silent without the hum of the refrigerator.

"Oh, dear," said Mom, "the power's out. Ellie, can you reach the flashlights and candles?" She pointed to the cupboard, and Ellie got them out.

Kimmy sneezed. Green stuff came out of her nose. Mom swiped a tissue across her face. "Poor baby," she murmured, "she's so uncomfortable.

Girls, do me a favor. Go play with Ryan. He's in the living room." Mom sounded distracted. She didn't look up when Nora and Ellie left. Kimmy kept swatting the tissue away.

Nora took the cheese sticks into the living room. "Ryan? Want a cheese stick?" she asked.

The living room was empty. Ryan's trucks lay in a pile on the floor.

"Where's Ry?" asked Ellie.

"I don't know." Nora shook her head.

"I'll find him," said Ellie. "He's *my* little brother." She put her hands on her hips.

Nora stuck out her chin. "Well, he's *my* cousin, so I can look if I want to."

Nora looked in the guest room and the bathrooms. No Ryan. He wasn't in Mom and Dad's bedroom, or Nora's room, or the garage.

Nora and Ellie ended up back in the living room. "Where could he be?" asked Nora.

"I'll bet he's hiding." Ellie looked behind the couch. "Ry? Where are you, bud?"

Nora opened the closet, remembering that he liked to play bear cave. Ryan wasn't there, but his cowboy boots lay on the floor. Covered in dried mud. Red mud. *Now why did that ring a bell?*

She fingered the boots thoughtfully. "Look," she told Ellie, "I've seen this kind of dirt before."

"You have? Where?"

"At the haunted house," said Nora slowly.

She stared out the window, into the storm. Leaves swirled along the ground and scattered in the air. Branches whipped back and forth. Fir cones thudded against the window. A garbage can blew over and clattered down the street.

"Do you think he's there?" asked Nora. "At the haunted house?"

Ellie turned on her, angrily. "If he is, it's your fault!" she snapped. "*You* told him to go back to Texas."

"Well, *you* told him to get lost!" Nora shoved her hands in her pockets.

"You said you didn't want us here." Ellie narrowed her eyes.

Nora shook her head. "We don't have time to argue," she said. "Ryan might be in danger!"

15
Where Is Ryan?

"I'm gonna go find him," said Ellie. "And I don't need any help from you." She ran out the front door.

Nora stopped just long enough to yell to Mom. "We're going after Ryan!" She ran out after Ellie. The wind slammed the door behind her.

The force of the wind made it almost too hard to walk. Nora pushed against it, following Ellie to the haunted house. All around, branches whipped past them. The empty house loomed ahead of them. Bleak. Forbidding.

Ellie stopped so suddenly that Nora ran into her. The hole under the porch yawned like an open mouth in the red mud. A hungry mouth.

The bear cave. It was probably wet. Probably cold. Almost certainly filled with creepy-crawly spiders.

Could Ryan be down there? Nora remembered how he liked to hide. How he liked to play bear cave. How interested he'd been in the haunted house. *What if he was there? What if he was hurt?*

Nora climbed across a fallen branch. She crept up to the edge of the hole. Wooden stairs led down into the gloom. "Ryan?" she called. The only answer was the roar of the wind.

Ellie followed close behind. She stood next to Nora, peering down the steps. "You first," she whispered. Nora turned, surprised.

Ellie's eyes burned like holes in her white face. "It's dark." Her voice was so quiet that Nora had to lean close to hear above the storm. "I didn't know it would be so dark."

Ellie—the Texas Terror—was scared!

Wind whipped Nora's hair into her face as she hesitated at the top of the stairs. Just then, an eerie wail came from the basement, cutting through the noise of the storm. Nora froze. *Ghosts? Wild animals? Or Ryan?*

Nora took a deep breath. Ellie was scared. Well, so was she. But Ryan might be down there. *Alone!*

16
Gumption

"We can do this." Nora grabbed Ellie's hand. "Together," she said. Holding hands, they inched down the wooden steps.

The basement was dark and full of shadows. The only light came through a cracked window. Gray, cobwebby things hung from the beams above. *Spiders?* Nora hunched her shoulders.

The sound of the storm had faded. But the basement wasn't quiet. Creaks, groans, and bumps came from the house overhead. *The wind? Or ghosts?* Nora shivered.

The two girls crept through the shadowy space. "Ryan?" called Nora. "Where are you?" Her voice echoed. Ellie's hand felt clammy in hers.

A faint sound, as trembling as a kitten's mew, came from a corner. There, just visible in the dim light, they found Ryan. He was huddled on the floor, crying, wet, and covered in red mud.

"Ry-buddy!" cried Ellie. She swept him up in a hug. "What are you doing here? You know you aren't supposed to leave the house by yourself!" she scolded.

"He's hurt!" said Nora. Ryan's jeans were torn, and his knee was bloody. Nora dug a tissue out of her pocket and swiped at the blood. "We have to get him home."

For a few minutes, Ryan was crying too hard to talk. Then his sobs turned to hiccups. He put his arms around Ellie and Nora. "I was—" he hiccuped and started again. "I was playing bear cave," he said. "Like I did yesterday. Aunt Ruthie was busy with Kimmy. She didn't see me."

He looked down at his mud-covered bunny slippers. "I forgot my boots. But then—*CRASH!* A big branch fell down. I ran down here to hide. I fell down." He wiped his nose on the back of his hand. "What took you guys so long? I've been here for years!"

Nora smiled, but then grew serious. "Can you walk?" Ryan shook his head. "How are we going to get him up the stairs?" Nora asked Ellie.

Ellie held out her hands. "Grab my wrists and

I'll grab yours. I learned this in first aid." They made a chair out of their arms. "Up you go, Ryan," Ellie ordered. "Put your arms around our shoulders."

With Ryan sitting on their arms, the girls slowly climbed the stairs. Step by step. On the top step, they stopped to catch their breath. Ryan sat on the steps. Outside, the wind still gusted through the trees.

"We broke some rules," Nora said, rubbing her wrists.

"But we saved Ryan." Ellie held Ryan's hand.

"We did it together," said Nora. "What did Grandpa say? Gumption. We've got gumption."

"We make a good team," Ellie agreed.

"Team Eleanor," said Nora.

AAAOOOOWWW! Suddenly, spooky sounds came from the house. Weird howls, followed by snarling. And something—*or someone*—hissed.

"Ghosts!" cried Ryan. The cousins quickly scooped up Ryan and headed down the street for home.

They didn't see two raccoons streak out of the basement behind them.

Mom listened as they all tried to explain at once. She hugged Nora and Ellie and Ryan in spite of all the mud. She cleaned his bloody knee and bandaged it. Then she used the camping stove to make hot chocolate. The power was still out.

"Whipped cream for me," said Nora. She whispered because Kimmy was finally asleep.

Ellie made a face. "Not for me. I only like marshmallows."

"I want both," said Ryan.

"Dad called," said Mom, as she poured the hot chocolate. "The police are clearing the roads. Everyone will be home in a few hours."

Mom was so glad to see them all safe, she didn't say anything about the rules they had broken. "Your grandmother would be proud of you," she told the girls. Then she put her hands on her hips and gave them a stern look. "But you are all absolutely forbidden to go near that place again. Ever."

That was just fine with Nora.

17

Hot Dogs—but No Relish

Over the weekend, Nora and Ellie finished their family history project. Ellie remembered the answers Grandpa had given to the interview questions. Nora wrote them down in her tidy handwriting. Ellie drew a border around the report, with pictures of the whole family. They both filled in the family tree, adding branches until both families fit.

Things went better. Ellie tried to keep her stuff picked up. Nora didn't nag. Nora peeled up the duct-tape line. Fuzzy didn't escape again. Even the crickets sounded soothing.

At school, the new desk had finally arrived. Now, Nora didn't have to share. Having enough space for her knees was a relief. But Nora found she missed Ellie. Once they'd stopped arguing, it had been fun to sit together. They had started passing notes, addressed "To Eleanor" and signed, "From Eleanor" to mystify their classmates.

Near the end of October, Ellie and Nora turned in their family history project. They did their oral report on why they had the same name, taking turns to share the story of the two stubborn sisters. Everyone laughed. Mr. Baldwin gave them a B+.

At home, Fuzzy still acted strange. Ellie spent hours staring into the tank. Nora sat beside her. Oddly enough, now that she'd seen Fuzzy close up, Nora found that the sight of the tarantula didn't scare her as much as it used to.

"Is she dying?" asked Nora, surprised she could feel even a little bit sorry for a spider.

Ellie shook her head. "She's molting. I read about it in a book. When tarantulas outgrow their skin, they shed. Like snakes."

Ryan came in, and they all watched as Fuzzy pulled herself out of her old skin, revealing her new skin. Her brownish-pink bristles shone like copper. She moved as gracefully as a dancer, putting one leg delicately down before lifting the next. Ellie took Fuzzy's old skin to school for show-and-tell.

One Thursday night, everyone gathered around the dinner table eating stew and biscuits. Uncle Chad's cell phone rang. "Excuse me," he said, leaving the room.

Uncle Chad was gone a long time. When he came back, he was grinning.

"Good news!" he exclaimed. "You're looking at the new technology specialist for the city of Klamath Falls."

Everyone began to talk at the same time.

"Wonderful!" Aunt Becca put her head on Uncle Chad's shoulder. Nora thought she had tears in her eyes.

"Good daddy," commented Ryan, taking another biscuit.

"Now can we go get Sue and Bubba?" asked Ellie.

"Klamath Falls!" said Mom. "That's only about six hours away."

"I'll start looking for a place right away," said Aunt Becca. "We can hire a moving van to bring our furniture."

"Sue and Bubba?" reminded Ellie.

Aunt Becca smiled. "Of course! First thing!"

"The pay isn't what I was making," Nora heard Uncle Chad tell Dad, "but it's steady work."

Kimmy pounded on her tray with delight.

Only Nora didn't say anything. She watched as everyone around her laughed and talked and planned.

It was good news, of course. Now Ellie would

have a place to live again, and Nora would have her own room back. No more arguing over the bathroom sink. No more sharing clothes. No more beans in the chili or meatballs in the sauce. And no more giant spider!

But think of all the things she'd miss. No more Ryan to read bedtime stories to. No more silly songs from Uncle Chad and hugs from Aunt Becca. No more whispering with Ellie after lights out. A lump rose in Nora's throat.

Ellie leaned over. She seemed to know what Nora was thinking. "It's only six hours away," Ellie said. "You can come visit. I want you to meet my dogs. They'll like you."

"We can meet at Silver Falls State Park for a picnic this summer!" said Nora. "That's about halfway."

"Hot dogs!" shouted Ryan.

"With relish," said Nora. "But no mustard."

"We can go hiking," said Ellie.

Nora made a face. "Swimming," she said. "Hiking's too sweaty."

Ellie put her hands on her hips. "In Texas, we go hiking on picnics."

Nora started to glare at her. But then she caught the twinkle in Ellie's eyes and laughed instead. "We'll do both," she said, nodding at her cousin.

Across the table, Mom took Aunt Becca's hand. "Sunshine and shadow," she said.

"Just like we were," Aunt Becca agreed.

"Stubborn as a team of mules," said Uncle Chad, shaking his head.

How to Be an Ancestor Detector
By Nora Robinson

A family history project can be a great way to learn about your ancestors. When Ellie and I talked to Grandpa, we found out things about our mothers that we hadn't known.

Grandpa says stories passed down from generation to generation keep family history alive. "Family stories give you a sense of belonging," he says. "They let you know your roots."

Mr. Baldwin says learning your family history can tell you:

- Where you come from
- Who you belong to
- What values are important in your family
- What ties your family together
- What makes your family unique

First Mr. Baldwin told us to make a family tree. You can draw your own or use a pattern from the Internet. Then we interviewed an ancestor. Here are some questions to get you started:

- What did you do when you were my age?
- Where did you go to school?
- What games did you play?
- Where did you grow up?
- Where else did you live?
- What was your first job?
- Where did you get married?

You can record the interview and type the answers later. You can even make a scrapbook with pictures and stories on each page.

Some kids in my class, like Jason, are adopted. Some of them wrote about their adopted families and some used their birth families. Jason did both of his families. Even though he complained about too much work, I think he was proud of having the biggest tree in the class.